P9-EAJ-111

JAMES PRELLER
SWAMP MONSTER
SCARY TALES

Illustrated by IACOPO BRUNO

WITHDRAWN

FEIWEL AND FRIENDS

New York

A FEIWEL AND FRIENDS BOOK
An Imprint of Macmillan

SWAMP MONSTER. Text copyright © 2015 by James Preller. Illustrations copyright © 2015 by Iacopo Bruno. All rights reserved. Printed in the United States of America by R. R. Donnelley & Sons Company, Harrisonburg, Virginia. For information, address Feiwel and Friends, 175 Fifth Avenue, New York, N.Y. 10010.

Feiwel and Friends books may be purchased for business or promotional use. For information on bulk purchases, please contact the Macmillan Corporate and Premium Sales Department at (800) 221-7945 x5442 or by e-mail at specialmarkets@macmillan.com.

Library of Congress Cataloging-in-Publication Data

Preller, James.
Swamp monster / James Preller ; illustrated by Iacopo Bruno. — First edition.
pages   cm. — (Scary tales ; 6)
Summary: Twins Lance and Chance LaRue are seeking a pet in the swamp near their Texas shack when they happen upon an egg and bring it home to hatch, but the creature's mother finds them, determined to rescue her little one.
ISBN 978-1-250-04097-8 (hardback) — ISBN 978-1-250-04523-2 (trade paperback) — ISBN 978-1-250-08020-2 (ebook) [1. Brothers—Fiction. 2. Twins—Fiction. 3. Monsters—Fiction. 4. Pets—Fiction. 5. Swamps—Fiction. 6. Horror stories.] I. Bruno, Iacopo, illustrator. II. Title.
PZ7.P915Sw 2015   [Fic]—dc23   2014049282

Book design by Ashley Halsey

Feiwel and Friends logo designed by Filomena Tuosto

First Edition: 2015

10 9 8 7 6 5 4 3 2 1

mackids.com

This book is dedicated to Jean and Liz.
I am forever grateful for the opportunity.

CONTENTS

THE WET
TRACES . . .

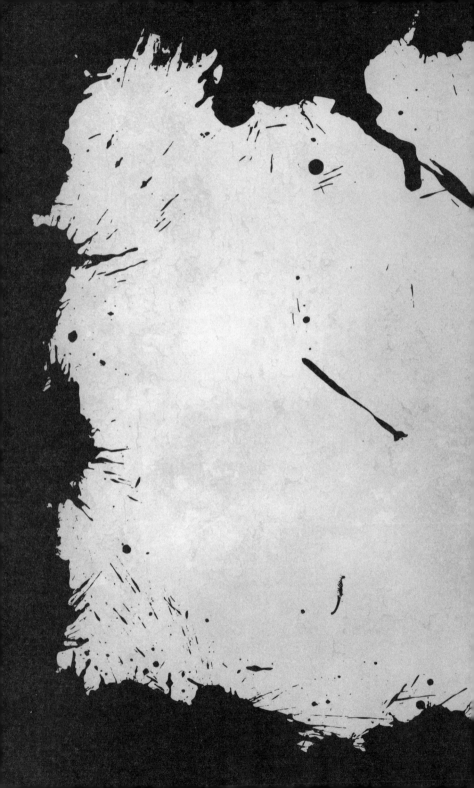

SQUILCH, SQUILCH, SQUILCH.

PLUNK, SPLAT, GLORP, SPLURGE . . .

The Dirge Chemical Plant had been dumping toxic sludge into the swamp for the past twenty-five years.

The illegal dumping was a fact well-known to the folks in Avarice County, but no one complained.

Because of course, they didn't.

Most of the waste leaked into remote swampland and drained into the good earth.

Out of sight, out of mind. Dirge Chemical was owned by the wealthiest family in the state. It employed more than five hundred hardworking men and women from all over the county. Folks depended on that plant for their survival. If it were shut down, they'd lose their jobs and their homes. And what then?

So when it came to a little bit of poison sludge oozing into the earth, folks looked the other way.

DRIP, DROP, SPLURK. It leaked into the streams and waterways, into ponds and lakes. Poison soaked into the ground.

What about the creatures of that environment? The fish and birds and snakes and gators? The animals that drank the water daily? That swam amidst the burbling toxins? Well, most died off. But some adapted. Mutated. Learned how to feed off the toxic waste. Those creatures grew stronger, bigger, tougher.

More dangerous, too.

The pollution was the worst out on the Dead River, which ebbed into Dismal Swamp like a last, dying gasp. Hardly anybody lived out there. Nobody important. Some poor folks, mostly. And that's where our story begins—with two boys, Lance and Chance LaRue. On this day, they were knee-deep in the foul, nasty water, swiping at mosquitoes, searching for frogs.

That was their first mistake.

SWAMP PET

Chance and Lance were brothers, and twins. They both had narrow faces, pointy noses, large eyes, and long, yellow hair that had never seen a comb. Half the time Chance and Lance even shared each other's clothes, inside out and *still* muddy.

Chance was the firstborn, the oldest by three minutes, and still in a hurry. Lance was the twin with a chipped front tooth and worried eyes. That's how people told them apart.

"Chance is the lively one," their mother would say. "Lance always looks like he thinks a piano is about to fall on his head. Hasn't happened yet, though, and I'm mighty glad of that. Them pianos are expensive to repair."

Then she'd laugh and laugh, holding her round belly.

It was true. Lance was prone to accidents. Lance was the one who spilled milk, got splinters, sat in poison ivy, and got stung by bees. If Lance stood next to Chance in a thunderstorm, Lance would surely be the one who got struck by lightning. Chance wouldn't even get wet.

Even so, despite these differences—or perhaps because of them—the two brothers loved each other fiercely. Maybe it was the hard times that bonded the boys together. Life was not easy at home. They were dirt poor and lived in a falling-down, two-story shack their daddy had hammered together long ago behind Dismal Swamp. And there it remained, sagging into the mud, drained of color by the hot Texas sun. Home, sweet home. Even worse, their daddy had a habit of disappearing for long stretches at a time. Out hunting, or away with friends, or locked up in jail somewhere. Mama said he was a "ne'er-do-well." Chance and Lance didn't know what that meant, exactly, but they figured it was another way of saying "good for nothing."

Sad, but true.

On this sweltering summer morning, the boys headed deep into the shaded swampland. Chance carried a metal bucket in the hopes they might capture some critter worth keeping. That was a constant pursuit for the boys—they longed for a pet. Once the twins found a stray dog, and begged their mother to keep it. She replied, "Boys, I can barely feed you two, ain't no way we can take in another hungry mouth," and that was that. No dog. End of story.

The muddy path skirted the edge of the swampy water. Fortified by peanut butter sandwiches—no jelly to be found at home—the boys felt strong and adventurous. They went deeper into the woods than usual. The trees thickened around them, with names like black willow and water hickory. Long limbs hung low. Spanish moss dangled from the branches like exotic drapes. Snakes slithered. Water rats lay still and watched through small, red eyes. Once in a while, a bird called. Not a song so much as a warning.

STAY AWAY, GAWK, STAY AWAY!

The farther the boys traveled, the darker it got.

Lance stopped and slapped a mosquito on the back of his neck. The bug exploded, leaving behind a splash of blood. "I don't know,

Chance," he said doubtfully. "Getting dark, getting late."

Chance chewed on a small stick. He spat out a piece of bark. "Let's keep on going." And off he went, leading the way, content that Lance would follow.

After another while, Chance paused and stooped low, bringing his eyes close to the ground. He pointed to a track in the mud. "What you think, Lance?"

"Too big for a gator," Lance said. He turned to gaze into the dark, snake-infested water as if staring into a cloudy crystal ball. "But I'd say it's gator-ish."

"Heavy, too," Chance noted. "You can tell 'cause the print sank way down."

"Guess you're right," Lance agreed.

"Here's another," Chance said, moving two steps to his right. "Three clawed toes, webbed feet. Weird."

"Never seen the likes of it before," Lance

said. "Looks like it was moving fast, judging by the length of the stride—"

"—and headed right there," Chance said, pointing to the swamp, "into the water."

"You reckon those tracks were made by Bigfoot?" Lance asked.

Chance grinned at his brother. They both laughed until the swamp swallowed up the sound. They stood together in the echo of that lonely silence.

"Maybe we should head back," Lance suggested.

"I suppose," Chance said, a little mournfully. "Hold on a minute." He pointed to a hollow by the edge of the water. "Is that an egg?"

"Good eyes, Chance. Turtle egg maybe," Lance confirmed.

Chance inspected it. Cocked his head, listened, looked around. No creature stirred.

"Let's take it home with us," he said.

"It don't feel right," Lance said. "That's some critter's baby."

"It'll be fine," Chance said. "You and me, we'll be real good mamas."

Lance snickered. "I'm not no mama—that's your job, Chance. I'll be the papa."

And that was that. Chance made a bed of mud, twigs, and leaves in the bottom of the bucket. He gently lifted the egg and placed it inside.

"Carry that real soft," Lance advised. "Like a sweet, nice mama."

In response to that, Chance gave his twin a quick kick in the pants.

"Hey!" Lance protested. He pushed Lance in the chest.

"Hey nothing," Chance replied. "Don't start messing around, I don't want this egg to crack."

Right, the egg. Lance peeked into the bucket. The egg was unharmed. So the boys headed home, stealing away with their curious prize through the gathering dark.

THE LITTLE MONSTER

Lance lay awake that night in the cramped, stuffy, upstairs room he shared with his brother. A clattering fan pointlessly pushed the hot air around. During the summer, the room felt like an oven. The twin boys baked in bunk beds—with Chance up top, tossing and murmuring and kicking in his sleep. Lance flipped over his pillow, seeking the cool side. Shirtless, he cast aside his only blanket, a thin sheet. The room smelled like a mixture of swamp, sweat, and soggy socks.

Darkness filled the room. It felt like a presence, a living thing that came to spend the night, watchful in a corner, waiting. Lance breathed in the dark. It filled his lungs, entered his stomach. He closed his eyes and the darkness waited. He opened them and it seemed to smile. The invisible night's sharp teeth. Lance breathed out. He disliked the long nights when the sounds of Dismal Swamp played like an eerie orchestra in the air. Frogs croaking, bugs buzzing . . . and the sudden, startled cry of a rodent killed by some winged creature in the night.

Lance rolled over, placing his bare feet on the floor. He turned on the reading lamp. There was a *Dark Knight* comic book on the floor where he had let it slip from his fingers. Bruce Wayne, the Batman!

He heard something. A **TAP-TAP-TAPPING**. Lance crept on silent feet to the closet and slid out the metal pail. On his knees, Lance peered at the egg inside.

"Chance," Lance whispered. "Chance, quick. Come see this."

Chance moaned and rolled away to face the wall.

"It's hatching!"

That got Chance's full attention. He sat up and, with an athletic thump, landed on the ground.

"I was dreaming about Dad—"

"Shhh," Lance interrupted. "Listen . . . it's coming."

TAP, TAP, HISSSSS.

A crack formed across the top of the shell. It spider-webbed into a network of cracks. A small, dark claw poked through. It tore away pieces of shell, bit by bit. The boys watched

in awe. Finally, the creature was revealed. It was moist and dark and stood shakily on two uncertain legs. It had two large, yellow eyes and the thick skin of a gator, with a raised ridge along its spine. The twins saw that it had webbed feet with three clawed toes.

"That ain't no turtle," Chance said.

"Nope," Lance agreed. "Look at those claws, those teeth. I've never seen nothing like it before. What do you think it is, Chance?"

"I sure don't know," the oldest boy replied. "But I'll tell you what. I don't *ever* want to meet the chicken that laid that egg."

At that moment, the newborn raised itself to full height, about six inches. With an angry hiss, the creature opened its mouth wide like a boa. A blood-red neck frill rattled open. **SPLAT, SPLATTER!** The creature spat black gobs of goo against the side of the pail.

"Whoa, it's a monster," Lance whispered in a soft, appreciative voice. "Our very own swamp monster."

And with those words, the two boys stared at each other . . . and high-fived.

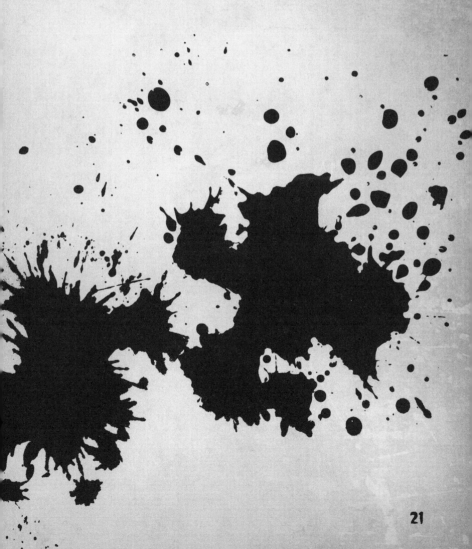

ROSALEE SERENA RUIZ

Chance and Lance found a spot in the woods where their new pet would stay out of harm's way. There was no need for their mother to know. She'd make them dump it in the woods somewhere. Or maybe she'd want to cook it in a soup.

So in secret, the twins nailed together a mishmash of found objects (junk, mostly) to build a cage. It included an old plastic swimming pool in the center, which they filled halfway with water. To this they added random wooden planks, wire, rocks, and plants. In the end, they had built a fabulous new home for their one special resident.

They even gave the creature a name, too: *Thing*. Just that, no more. Thing.

Most times, the creature was quiet and gentle, like a baby. It grew to trust Lance, and allowed the boy to hold it and whisper to it gently. Lance beamed down a chipped-tooth smile. He cooed, "Hey, sweet Thing. You're a good little pet."

It liked the water, and stayed under the surface for hours at a time. But Thing did have a nasty side. Once it nearly snapped Chance's index finger right off. Would have, too, if it wasn't for Chance's quick reflexes.

Finding the right food for Thing was also a problem. The boys discussed it at length: *What do you feed a little monster?*

It was hard to answer. They tried different foods from home—chips and pretzel sticks and orange pop—but most foods didn't work. Thing did eat half a hamburger once, but those were scarce. One day, the boys found the half-eaten corpse of a dead chipmunk in Thing's cage.

Chance scratched his head. "How you figure that got in here?"

"Climbed, I guess," Lance replied. "You think Thing killed it? And ate it?"

"I know plenty of cats would do the same thing," Chance replied, nonjudgmentally. "It's nature. Everybody eats everybody else. That's how the world works."

"Guess you're right," Lance nodded.

The boys did not discuss what might happen when their little monster grew into a big monster? What would it eat then?

Or *whom*?

They didn't hear Rosalee Serena Ruiz sneak up on them.

"What you got there?" she asked.

They had been found out. There was no use trying to hide it from Rosalee—or Rosie, as they called her. If someone had to discover their secret, Rosalee was the best person for it. She could spit farther, burp louder, run faster, and snap thick branches across her knee. Rosalee was a girl all right, but the boys didn't mind. In fact, they barely noticed. To them, she was just a cool kid.

Rosie was a grade older and lived two minutes down the gravel road. Thick black hair, brown eyes, smooth chocolate skin, dimples, cutoff jeans, and a NASCAR T-shirt: Perfect in every way. Rosie's father could fix most anything—from toasters to TV sets—and he passed that gift onto his only daughter. Rosie knew her way around car engines and wore the grease stains to prove it.

The boys never spoke of it, but they agreed: Rosie was the most beautiful girl they'd ever seen. They would do anything to see her smile.

"I swung by your place," Rosalee said, "but the blinds were drawn. I figured your mom might still be sleeping, so I didn't knock."

"You figured right," Chance said, approving of the girl's caution.

Rosalee nodded her chin at Thing. "What y'all got there?"

"Used to be an egg," Lance offered. He gestured toward the woods. "We found it in there, yonder, deep a-ways. Brought it back here. Now it's . . . it's . . . whatever this is."

"We named it Thing," Chance clarified.

"Thing," Rosie repeated. She eased herself

down on her knees and stared at the creature, nose to nose.

It was the strangest creature Rosie had ever seen. It stood on two legs like a reptile man, though with a gator's tough skin and the powerful jaw of a snapping turtle. It had three claws on each foot, joined by webs. A long fin, like a sail, ran along its spine.

HISS.

"Careful now, Rosie," Lance warned. "Back up."

Thing's neck frill rattled and spread open.

HISSSSSS!

Lance quickly placed his hand out to shield Rosie's face.

SPLAT! A gob of black liquid shot forth from Thing's mouth, splattering against the back of Lance's hand. Lance cried out

in pain, "Gosh darn, not again! That burns, Thing!" He clutched the injured hand tight to his chest.

"You all right?" Rosie asked.

"He's fine. Stings like prickers, that's all," Chance said.

"It goes numb like a bad spider bite," Lance complained, rubbing the hand. "Lasts just a few minutes. I've felt worse than this lots of times."

Rosie stared in wonder at the captured creature. "That was completely gross . . . and waaay cool. It shoots poison?"

"Uh-huh," Lance said.

"Yup," Chance agreed.

"Tell me everything," Rosie demanded.

So they told Rosie the entire tale. She listened carefully. Asked a few questions. Listened some more.

Finally, Rosie announced, "I want to

bring it home with me. Give it a proper place to live."

The twins glanced at each other, read each other's thoughts without speaking a word.

"I don't know," Lance said.

"It's ours," Chance stated.

"We can share it," Rosalee suggested. "I'll keep it at my house on rainy days."

"I guess," Lance agreed. After all, there was no sense arguing with Rosalee Serena Ruiz. Who'd even want to?

"Tell you what," Chance said. "Tomorrow, we'll go find an egg for you."

Rosalee's dimpled face brightened into a huge smile. "And I'm coming with y'all! Because guess what? I know where we can get a boat."

THUNDER IN THE WOODS

The next morning before the birds woke up, the three explorers headed back to Dismal Swamp.

"I had an Uncle Edgardo who used to hunt gators," Rosie told the boys as they walked. "He'd tell us stories. He said some men went deep into Dismal Swamp and never returned. A lady, too, some years back."

"Like they drowned?" Lance asked.

"Eaten by gators, I bet," Chance mused. "*Chomp, chomp.*"

"Gross!" Rosie gave Chance a punch on the shoulder for that one, even though she laughed. "All I know is what I heard," she said. "It's a dangerous place. Real polluted. Smells awful. They say there's strange creatures live out here, like nothing nobody has ever seen."

The path started out firm and dry. But as they drew deeper into the heart of the dark land, it grew wet and sludgy. Chance led the way.

Rosalee paused, looking around.

"This way," Chance said. "Still a-ways to go."

"I remember this place. There," Rosie pointed to the left, in the direction of Dead River. "Uncle Edgardo used to stash his boat down this other way, I think."

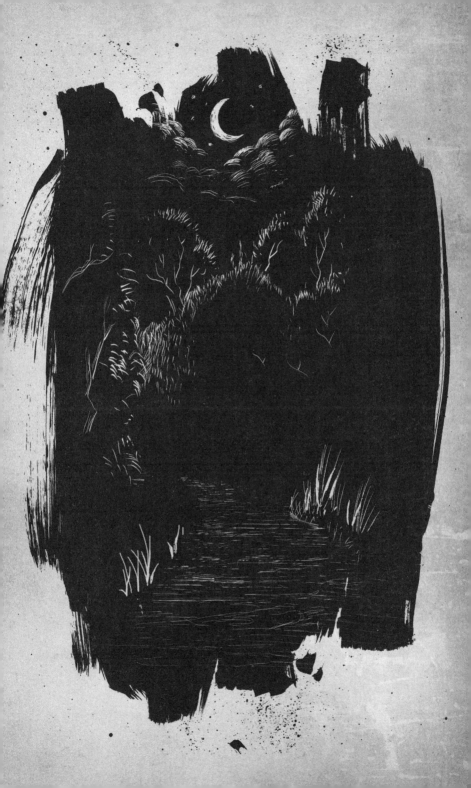

"Ain't you sure?" Chance asked.

Rosie shook her head. "I haven't been back here in a few years, ever since Uncle Edgardo disappeared."

"What?" Lance said. "He disappeared, too?"

"There's bad things in these woods," Rosie explained. "Snakes and such. My father says he likely ran off with a pretty waitress. Who knows what happened. You two wait here. I'll scout ahead down this bitty side path, take a little look."

Rosie pushed ahead down the barely-there path.

"I don't want to get lost," Lance confided to his brother.

"Like Hansel and Gretel in the woods," Chance replied. "We might get cooked in a pie!"

Lance frowned. "The witch tried to cook

them in an oven—but there weren't no pie that I recall."

A moment later, Rosie called out, "I found it! The Dead River, and my uncle's boat!"

They followed the sound of her voice and soon stared at a battered, old, upside-down canoe. It had been pulled ashore and propped up against a tree. Vines grew over it, like the arms of a green octopus. Two paddles lay on the ground beside it.

"I sure don't know about this," Lance said, doubtfully.

"Aw, it'll be fun," Chance stated. And soon enough, they were floating in the canoe on the Dead River that trickled, ever so slowly, into Dismal Swamp. Lance and Chance paddled. Rosie sat in the front.

The river was still, nearly stagnant. It was hardly a river at all. More like a tired, old body of water that only wanted to lie down and sleep. It stank of decay and rotted leaves. Once in a while, a bird called. A faint splash signaled an animal entering the water, a gator or water rat or who knows what. The leaves of a bush trembled for an instant, quivering in the stillness.

It was, to the twins, a silence that felt like danger, of bad things about to happen. "Somebody got it right when they named this place Dismal," Lance observed. A feeling of dread burrowed deep into his bones.

Still the boys paddled on, carving through the dark, shallow water.

At last, they entered Dismal Swamp. Lance rested the paddle across his lap. He tilted his head.

"You tired already, brother?" Chance teased.

"Shhh. Hear that?" Lance whispered.

Rosie and Chance leaned forward, aching

to hear. **CRACK, CRACK, SPLASH!** It was the sound of distant thunder. Lance looked up through a small gap in the overhanging trees. The sky was clear. Not a cloud. Then another sound reached them, a sound that was hard to describe. It was like a mournful song, a desolate groan—wind in the darkness—carrying all the sorrow of the world in its arms.

"I have a bad feeling," Rosie said, turning around. The boys saw Rosie's white, ghostlike face. She shivered. And because of that—because of what they saw in her eyes—Lance and Chance felt a sharp jab of fear, too.

CRACK again, louder this time. Nearer. And again came the high-pitched, waterlogged, pitiful cry.

OOOOOOH, OOOOOOH.

Chance whispered, "Whatever's making that noise, it's just up around the bend, beyond those mangrove trees. I say we tie off. I don't like it out here on the open water."

A pull of the paddle, then another, and the boat eased into the shore, obscured by a blanket of hanging moss.

"Let's sneak up real quiet," Chance said.

"And watch out for snakes, Rosie," Lance warned. "The yellow-backed ones can kill you with just one bite."

THE CREATURE OF
THE SWAMP

They picked their way through the boggy muck. Sometimes a foot squished deeply into the mud, as if gripped by the earth. When a foot got stuck in the ground, it only came loose with a hard yank, followed by a sucking sound, **_thwuuck-wuuffft_**. Most times the three explorers climbed cautiously along the slippery roots of mangroves.

Chance led the way, his blood humming,

going **thrum-thrum-thrum**. As they scrambled forward, the cries grew louder. The sounds were full of violence and pain, as if made by a wounded animal.

And then—there, through a tangle of moss, across the swampy water—they spied it.

The creature of the swamp.

It could not be real.

No way.

Impossible.

And yet, there it stood.

Lance, Rosie, and Chance huddled close in a tangle of arms and legs. No one spoke. They stared in silent terror.

The creature was covered in moss and blisters, bumps and nasty sores. It had the shape of a man: a giant or a circus freak, but like no man of this earth.

A mutant—part gator, part fish, part beast.

They had never seen anything like it. Except for once before, back home, in a hand-made cage.

For clearly, this horrible creature was related to Thing.

The monster beat its scaly chest. It cried in a groan of agony. It easily snapped a thick limb from the tree—CRACK!—and hurled the branch into the boggy water.

It stomped and raged.

And suddenly, as a breeze kicked up, it stopped.

And sniffed.

And looked warily around.

"Shhh," Chance said needlessly, for no one dared speak. Rosie trembled, shaking with fear. Lance took her hand, tugged. *This-a-way*, he gestured. Slow and easy.

Rosie nodded and gripped Lance's hand tighter.

Chance stumbled on a root, ripping open a bloody gash of flesh. "Ow!" he groaned out loud.

Lance quickly covered his twin's mouth.

Three sets of young eyes stared out through the underbrush. Now the creature was hunched low, like a catcher in a baseball game, one clawed forelimb touching the ground. Its yellow eyes scanned the tree line. Searching, questioning.

In one smooth motion, it dove soundlessly into the water. Cool and gone. Hidden beneath the murky dark.

"I'm so scared," Rosie confessed. Her voice choked with fright.

"Let's go," Lance whispered, his voice soft, but clear. "Now."

"To the boat?" Chance asked.

Rosie shook her head, *No, no, no. Not back, not that way.*

Lance pointed in the opposite direction. Nodded once, looking to Chance for agreement.

Chance viewed the pathless muck. "Very messy, very slow," he said. "Let's do it."

UNDER THE WATER

The swamp creature, a female, sank through the water to the soft bottom. Eyes closed, she rolled her tongue back into her throat.

She felt safe in the cool wet.

Protected in the dark.

Unseen. Away from all eyes.

She breathed like a fish, through gills in her neck. Sometimes, she stayed under for hours, for days and weeks, and through the long months of winter, sleeping under a blanket of mud like a turtle.

With a subtle movement, she glided through the black water like a hawk riding the currents of the wind.

A thought troubled her mind.

Others were out there . . . Others had come to her home, her alone-place. She had sensed them, smelled them, seen them.

So she hid, as she always did.

She moved in the safe dark, the cool dark, and she grieved again for the egg that was gone. The child she never knew. That was her loss. And then slowly, painfully—like a cloud that gathers itself in the stormy sky—a new question formed in her skull.

Was the egg stolen?

Had it been taken . . . by the Others?

Those faces in the woods?

She had glimpsed them.

Their ugly, round eyes.

Their skin like smooth stones.

Little monsters.

New feelings began to stir inside the heart of the swamp creature.

Feelings of anger, of rage and revenge.

Her eyes opened, yellow in the black water.

With a push of her webbed feet, she rose like an arrow to the surface. Up to the air, to the afternoon light.

She would hunt them down, those pale faces in the woods.

She observed from the water, the way a gator cruises along the surface. Waiting, patient, watchful.

Where are you? she wondered.

And this thought came, too:

What have you done to my precious one?

THE HUNT

There was no clear path.

Lance, Chance, and Rosie moved through an area of shallow swamp water. A black and sodden mess of mud and slime.

"It smells awful here," Rosie said, holding a hand over her nose and mouth.

"No talking, not yet," Lance warned.

It was slow, moving through the swamp. Normally, Lance and Chance would never have taken this route. Not in a million years.

But the sight of that monster was fresh in their minds. It looked wild and dangerous, like an illustration from a bizarre comic book.

Small drops of blood dripped from the gash in Chance's knee. Rosie noticed. They paused. She scooped up a handful of mud and spread it across the wound. "There, nature's Band-Aid," she said.

They moved on, trudging step by step. Their feet sank into the shin-deep water, and at times, it felt as if the mud held them tight.

I WON'T LET GO, I WON'T LET GO. . . .

With a pull, a twist, a fierce yank, the foot was freed.

Thus they traveled: one step, one step, one step. Muscles ached and strained. They constantly slapped and scratched at mosquitoes. Weary, so weary. But their fright kept them plunging forward. They dared not pause to rest. They had to get far away from that thing . . . far from that monster back there.

"Hey, guys, um," Chance said, lagging behind. "I think I'm stuck. Can't seem to get my leg out."

A new cry filled the air, the horrible call of the swamp creature. It was far off, a distance away, but still out there somewhere. Hearts beating faster, Lance and Rosie grabbed Chance by the arms. They hauled and pulled.

THWUCK.

Chance's bare foot jerked free.

"My sneaker!" he exclaimed. He reached into the water, tried to free it from the mud. "It's caught on a root or something."

"Leave it, we don't have time," Lance said. "Up a bit, another fifty feet, there's dry land. We'll move faster soon."

Chance didn't argue. They were all on the edge of panic. Not a minute to waste.

Behind them, the swamp creature paused at the exact spot where the three children had huddled together. It was where she had first glimpsed them, hiding behind a curtain of moss. She smelled the boy's blood on the mangrove root. Tasted with her tongue the faintest slice of flesh that had been left from the boy's wound.

It was, the creature thought, delicious.

Fresh meat.

She followed on.

FULL DARK

It was raining in the full dark. The creature felt grateful for the rain. Water was her friend. Water was kind. She had never before come onto the Land of the Others. Some instinct had always told her to stay away. This place meant danger. So she waited in the declining twilight. She sat in stillness through the steady downpour. Like a chameleon: eyes shut, tongue rolled back, invisible in the thicket. The mother waited for night to wrap itself around her. The darkness, too, was her friend.

On the ground beside her lay Chance's muddy sneaker. She had found it, carried it all this way, following the scent. Hours earlier, she came across the structure the boys had built. The aroma filled her nostrils and at once she understood everything. Her very own had been here. The life that had been inside the egg. She felt new hope.

Thinking, *mine*.

But the cage was empty.

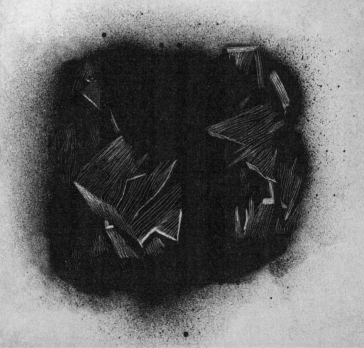

In a sudden fury, she destroyed it all. Smashed the boards, clawed deep gashes into the earth, cried out in rage.

Where are you, little one?

Finally at last, she stepped out of the woods. She sniffed the air, seeking the scent of her lost one. *Where, oh, where?* In the near distance stood a large structure. A dwelling place of the Others. She could smell them inside. The ones with faces as smooth as stones.

The egg stealers.

A cloud crossed before the moon.

The sky darkened.

It was time.

She stepped forward.

SQUILCH, SQUILCH, SQUILCH.

Fury in her heart.

And suddenly, the house went dark.

~~~

Their mother was out. On weekends, she worked the night shift at the 24-hour truck stop, where she poured coffee, served eggs, and always returned the next morning with a pocket jammed with dollar bills. Lance and Chance sat around a linoleum table in their small kitchen, eating crackers and slices of pepperoni. They were weary and still stunned by what they had seen.

"We shouldn't have let her take Thing tonight," Lance said.

Chance shrugged. "Maybe, maybe not. Rosie's a hard girl to say 'no' to. You know that, Lance. Plus, it's been raining hard."

"Thing likes water, rain don't bother it any," Lance protested.

"She'll take care of it. Rosie said she'll keep Thing safe in her shed," Chance reasoned. "We'll figure this out in the morning. We can't let things stay the way they are."

Lance shook his head. "I don't know."

"I'm too tired to argue," Chance replied. With a sharp knife, he cut the last hunk of pepperoni into two. He popped one slice into his mouth, and pushed the last piece toward Lance. A peace offering. Brothers. Share and share alike.

Lance checked the clock. Near midnight. He rose to bring the plate and two glasses to the sink. He'd wash them in the morning. He parted the curtains, peered out the window. "Still raining steady," he noted.

And then his heart skipped. He said: "What the—?"

Chance turned in his chair. He knew his brother well, every tone in his voice. "What is it?"

"I think I saw something," Lance said. "A shadow moving by the trees."

Chance came to the window. "Hard to see," he said. "Shut the light."

Lance flipped the wall switch. The room

went dark. And outside, under the night stars, they clearly saw a large, shadowy figure moving awkwardly toward the house.

SQUILCH, SQUILCH, SQUILCH.

"Upstairs, quick!" Chance ordered. He grabbed the knife off the table.

The boys bounded up the stairs in threes. By the time they reached the landing—**BOOM! CRUNCH!**—the front door flew open, knocked of its hinges.

The swamp monster stepped into the house.

THE CHASE

The creature stood wavering, confused, uncertain. For the first time in her life, she had ventured inside a man-made dwelling. This was not a natural place. It felt cold and hard. A shiver of doubt entered her mind.

———*w*w*———

SLAM!

Chance slammed the bedroom door. The boys quickly hauled a heavy dresser in front of it.

"Useless," Lance muttered.

"The window, brother," Chance said.

———

Stairs were a new problem. She had never before encountered a flight of stairs. There were not even hillsides in the swampland, which was flat. The stairs seemed too small for her webbed feet. But still, she climbed— **SQUILCH, SQUILCH, SQUELCH**—water dripping off her scales. *Plink*, *plink* on the wooden steps.

Up and up and up.

And then, confusion.

Nothing there.

The Others had vanished.

She heard a sound. She sensed they were

behind the door, though she had no word for door. No language for any of these things. "Door" was only an obstacle that separated her from what she wanted. The swamp creature had come for the Others. So she smashed through the door.

Honey, I'm home.

<hr />

Chance and Lance were long practiced in the art of sneaking out of the house. They had climbed out of their bedroom window dozens of times. But never this recklessly. Lance went first. He swung a foot over, then the other, and hung for a brief instant from the ledge. It was a good drop, and dangerous if he fell the wrong way. Easy to snap a leg or sprain an ankle. Lance had no time to worry about those things. He dropped and rolled onto the wet ground. Chance was

next. He paused, dangling by one hand, and with the other, closed the window.

Slipping, slipping.

"Geronimo!" he whispered.

He fell through the air and landed on a jagged rock. **Oomppff**, Chance collapsed to the ground. A jolt of pain shivered through his leg. Chance immediately knew that his ankle was broken.

The next moment, jagged shards of glass rained down from the sky. The window shattered.

A cry of bewildered pain came from the swamp monster. Blood and fury. The Others had escaped. Now the creature stood—raging, crazed, furious—inside the bedroom of Chance and Lance LaRue. Comic books scattered on the floor. Posters of Dallas Cowboys on the walls.

It turned, went out of the room, and tumbled down the stairs.

CAPTURED

"Run!" Lance exclaimed.

Chance hobbled forward a step and fell. "I can't, it's broken."

Lance pulled his twin to his feet, held Chance by the waist with one arm. He took Chance's left arm and wrapped it across his shoulders. "I've got you, Chance. We gotta move, we gotta move now!"

They only got about ten agonizing feet.

Then they heard it—the wheezing,

water-clogged breath of the swamp creature—and they knew it had found them
again.

"Go," Chance whispered to Lance. "Warn
Rosie. It came for the baby."

"I'm not leaving," Lance said.

"Save her," Chance ordered.

With a fierce shove, Chance pushed Lance
to the ground. He turned to face the creature.
It was bloodied from the window, battered
from its fall down the stairs. Injured and in
pain.

Chance hobbled forward on one good leg.
He clutched a knife in his right hand.

"Chance, no!"

"Just go!" Chance snapped. "Save Rosie.
Get Thing. It wants the baby!"

"No!" Lance roared back.

THWAP, SPLAT!

A spray of black bile hit —

Chance across the chest and face. He fell immediately, numb and unable to move. The knife, glittering in the moonlight, fell from his grip.

The creature stepped forward. Its yellow eyes now fixed on Lance.

It opened its mouth to spit.

Lance alertly dove and tumbled to the right.

Then he jumped up and ran, bent low, around to the back of the house.

The swamp creature watched the boy disappear into the night. Pieces of glass had pierced her thick, alligator skin. Blood leaked from her body. She turned her attention to the fallen one on the ground.

What to do, what to do?

The next instant, the porch light turned on. Lance raced outside—he had entered the house from the back door. He pounded together two metal pots.

BANG, CLANG, CLATTER!

The sounds were sharp and deafening.

Lance screamed and charged, "Arrrrrrghh!"

The noisy display startled the swamp creature, dizzy from the loss of blood. She reared back, confused, here in the Land of the Others. The sharp, unnatural noise blared in her eardrums. In a swift motion, she lifted up Chance and moved toward the woods—to the dark places, the hidden spaces. The monster carried the boy over her shoulder all the way back to Dismal Swamp.

THE HARD BARGAIN

Before the adults woke, Lance and Rosalee walked the muddy path.

They barely spoke.

Lance held the handle of a cat carrier he had borrowed from Rosalee. Thing was inside it, quietly unhappy.

Rosalee tried to put words to the bad feeling that gnawed at her belly. "What if, you know . . . ?"

Lance gritted his teeth. He stared forward. Kept walking. "He's alive. I *know* it."

"You can't be positive," Rosalee reasoned. "We have to make a plan that—"

"*I know it!*" Lance spat. He stopped in the middle of the path. "I feel him, Rosie. He's my twin. We're connected. Listen, I'm going out there and I'm not coming back until I bring him home. You can come with me or not, it won't change what I'm set to do."

Rosalee saw the conviction in his face. He looked fierce, powerful. "I'm coming," she said.

They walked past duckweed and cattails and possum haw, past water hickory and cypress trees. Rosie spied a heron in the shallow water, spearing a fish with its long beak. The day grew hot. They had not eaten. Lance did not pause to rest. He walked on. Rosie struggled to match the boy's determined pace.

At last, they came to the boat.

"What now?" Rosalee asked.

Lance didn't reply. He unlocked the cage,

reached in for Thing. The creature was quiet, watchful. Thing's eyes widened. It mewled, a soft sound. Lance placed the creature inside the boat.

"Stay put now," Lance whispered. "No swimming just yet. You're going home."

He moved waist deep into the foul, polluted water and pushed the boat across the swamp, to the place where they had first spotted the swamp creature.

Silence. Not a bird sang, not a creature stirred.

The boat slowly drifted to the opposite bank.

Lance and Rosalee watched, shoulder to shoulder.

With a jerk, the boat came to a stop at the far shore. A gentle breeze kicked up. Spanish moss—what the locals call "tree hair"—swayed from the branches.

And out she stepped, as Lance knew she would. The proud creature of the swamp. The mother moved to the boat and tenderly, lovingly, lifted Thing into her arms.

Lance stepped out into plain sight.

"Fair's fair," he called out.

The mother gazed at Lance through yellow eyes. They stood for a long moment, two creatures from different worlds, working out their differences. A sudden turn and she was gone. The swamp monster and her child retreated back into the safe, dark places.

More silence, more waiting.

Lance did not move.

"Lance?" Rosalee whispered.

"I ain't moving," he said. "I'll stand here forever if I have to."

Long minutes slithered by. Bugs buzzed and bit. Time passed on the swamp. Lance made no move.

And then, movement in the trees. He appeared. Chance hobbled toward the boat, looking haggard and ill. He gazed across the water at Lance and gave a half smile. He lifted a finger in greeting, and fell into the boat.

Somehow, Chance mustered the strength to give three pulls on the paddle, enough to move the craft across the still water.

As soon as the boat reached him, Lance hugged his twin. Rosalee climbed onto the boat, checking his wounds. "He's gonna be all right," she said to Lance. "His ankle's swelled up real bad, black and blue. We need to get him to a doctor."

"I know it," Lance said.

Chance raised a weakened hand. Lance took it in his, then squeezed.

"Thanks, brother," Chance said through dry, sun-chapped lips.

Lance nodded. "You'd do the same for me."

"We best not let Mom find out about this," Chance said, his soft voice like a rustle in the trees. Somehow he managed a sly grin.

"She'd never believe us anyhow," Lance replied.

"We'll have some explaining to do," Chance said. "We kind of left the house in a mess."

"Guess you're right," Lance said.

"Doors and windows can be fixed," Rosalee said. "But family, that's forever."

The two boys grinned, together again, the way they liked it. Twins forever connected. Brothers.

And somewhere in the unseen swamp, a mother and her little one swam together for the first time in the safe dark, the good dark.

My baby, she thought.

My very own.

SO THERE YOU HAVE IT. A TENDER
TALE OF TWO FAMILIES.

LOVELY, WASN'T IT?

AND NOT SO SCARY, RIGHT?

LANCE AND CHANCE LARUE
WERE TWO ORDINARY BOYS. A
LITTLE MISCHIEVOUS, BUT HARDLY
MONSTERS.

AND THAT MAMA IN THE SWAMP?
SHE SURE LOVED HER BABY TO
DEATH. SO WHAT IF SHE WAS
COVERED IN SCALES AND BLISTERS,
WITH YELLOW EYES AND SHARP
CLAWS?

OF COURSE, LANCE AND CHANCE
SHOULD HAVE NEVER TAKEN THAT
EGG. IT'S NOT A GOOD IDEA TO
COME BETWEEN ANY MOTHER AND
HER CHILD. ESPECIALLY THIS ONE.

SHE SPITS POISON WHEN SHE'S ANGRY.

BUT HERE'S THE QUESTION: WHO WAS THE REAL MONSTER IN THIS SCARY TALE?

THAT'S FOR YOU TO DECIDE.

SQUILCH, SQUILCH, SQUILCH.

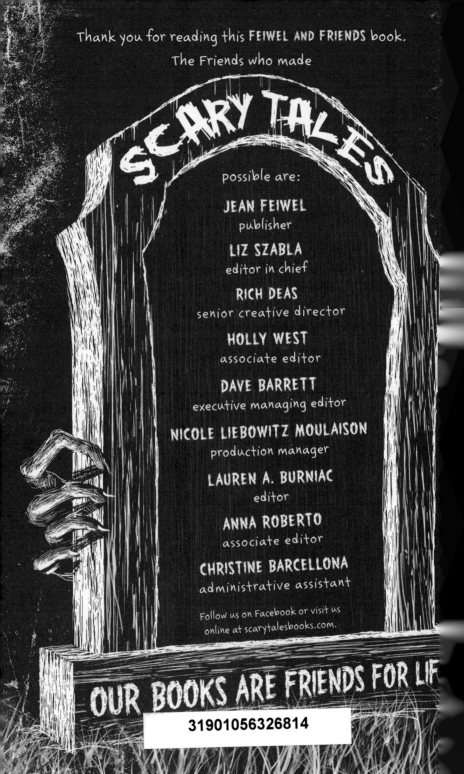

Thank you for reading this FEIWEL AND FRIENDS book.
The Friends who made

SCARY TALES

possible are:

JEAN FEIWEL
publisher

LIZ SZABLA
editor in chief

RICH DEAS
senior creative director

HOLLY WEST
associate editor

DAVE BARRETT
executive managing editor

NICOLE LIEBOWITZ MOULAISON
production manager

LAUREN A. BURNIAC
editor

ANNA ROBERTO
associate editor

CHRISTINE BARCELLONA
administrative assistant

Follow us on Facebook or visit us
online at scarytalesbooks.com.

OUR BOOKS ARE FRIENDS FOR LIF

31901056326814